Surfing and Other
EXTREME WATER SPORTS

Drew Lyon

raintree
a Capstone company — publishers for children

Raintree is an imprint of Capstone Global Library Limited, a company incorporated in England and Wales having its registered office at 264 Banbury Road, Oxford, OX2 7DY – Registered company number: 6695582

www.raintree.co.uk
myorders@raintree.co.uk

Edited by Anna Butzer
Designed by Cynthia Della-Rovere
Media research by Kelly Garvin
Original illustrations © Capstone Global Library Limited 2020
Production by Katy LaVigne
Originated by Capstone Global Library Ltd
Printed and bound in India

978 1 4747 9363 6 (hardback)
978 1 4747 9682 8 (paperback)

Acknowledgements
We would like to thank the following for permission to reproduce photographs: Alamy: Allan Seiden/Pacific Stock/Design Pics Inc, 22, Stephen Frink Collection, 10; Associated Press/Hugo Silva/Red Bull Content Pool, 5; Getty Images: Craig Pulsifer, 16, Stefan Matzke-sampics/Corbis, 7; iStockphoto/Richinpit, cover, back cover; Newscom/DENIS BALIBOUSE/REUTERS, 24; Shutterstock: Anna Moskvina, 14, C Levers, 12 (top), EpicStockMedia, 9, 19, Jeff Whyte, 27, Konstantin Faraktinov, 12 (middle right), Roberto Caucino, 29, Sing5pan, 12 (bottom), Vaclav Mach, 12 (middle left), wavebreakmedia, 13, Yulia Melnikova, 21. Artistic elements: Shutterstock: Edu Silva 2ev, nattanan726, pupsy

Every effort has been made to contact copyright holders of material reproduced in this book. Any omissions will be rectified in subsequent printings if notice is given to the publisher.

All the internet addresses (URLs) given in this book were valid at the time of going to press. However, due to the dynamic nature of the internet, some addresses may have changed, or sites may have changed or ceased to exist since publication. While the author and publisher regret any inconvenience this may cause readers, no responsibility for any such changes can be accepted by either the author or the publisher.

Contents

Chapter 1
Sweet dreams 4

Chapter 2
What is surfing? 8

Visual glossary. 12

Chapter 3
Wakeboarding 14

Chapter 4
Windsurfing 18

Chapter 5
Cliff diving 22

Chapter 6
How to make a start. 26

Glossary 30
Find out more 31
Index .32

Sweet dreams

Sometimes, when it's least expected, dreams come true. In 2017, pro surfer Rodrigo Koxa rode the wave of a lifetime in Nazaré, Portugal. On the eve of a competition at Nazaré Beach, Koxa's dream brought visions of a huge wave.

"I had an amazing dream the night before, where I was talking to myself: 'You gotta go straight down. You gotta go straight down,'" said Koxa, who started surfing at the age of five. "I didn't really know what it meant. But I decided somebody was talking to me. It was amazing."

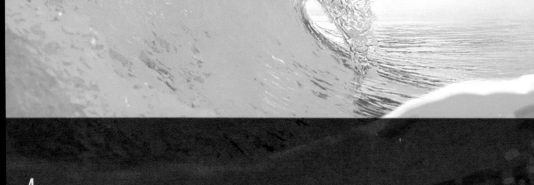

Rodrigo Koxa (right) surfs a big wave in Nazaré, Portugal, in 2017.

Koxa's dream became reality at Nazaré when he set the world record for the largest wave ever surfed. The massive wave measured 24 metres high, 61 centimetres higher than the previous record. A wave this epic only comes once – if you're lucky. It took less than a minute for Koxa to complete the ride.

But Koxa's moment in the sun almost never happened. A few years before his record-setting triumph, a **gnarly** wave in Nazaré nearly killed Koxa. His confidence had been crushed. The close call led to nightmares and Post-Traumatic Stress Disorder (PTSD). Koxa lost the courage and desire to surf.

After a year, Koxa overcame his fears with support from friends and family. When he returned to surfing, Koxa shied away from big **swells**. He started small before attempting to ride the bigger waves.

Koxa's historic wave in Portugal wasn't the first record-setter of his career. In 2010, he surfed the largest wave recorded in South America, an 18-metre swell.

By 2018, Koxa was at the top of the surfing world. The stunning video capturing his record ride quickly spread on social media. Setting a world record, Koxa later said, was the best day of his life.

"(The record) makes me feel proud and humble all at once," he said. When a chance to make history came his way, Rodrigo Koxa was ready.

gnarly large, nasty
swell large wave with a long, continuous crest

CHAPTER 2

What is surfing?

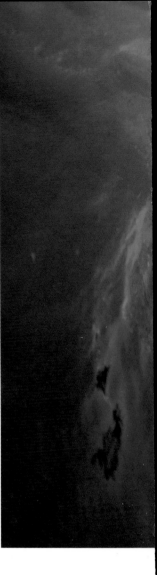

More than 70 per cent of Earth's surface is water. Many daredevil athletes leave the safety of land sports for natural thrills on water. Some water sports – such as surfing – don't require expensive equipment or gadgets. A decent board and big waves are all surfers need for a successful day on the water.

Surfing was invented by Polynesians. Samoans surfed on wooden planks thousands of years ago. European explorers witnessed surfing as early as the 1700s.

In time, surfing exploded into a worldwide hobby. Surfing became popular in California in the United States during the 1960s. From the Pacific Ocean, surfing culture spread across America and the world.

In surfing, the waves are in charge. A wave is a coach, teammate and referee. It's never the opponent. Surfers ride with a wave, not against it. But surfers don't follow a scoreboard. They don't watch a clock either. Time seems to stop when you're surfing.

Athletes who don't live near the sea can practise in artificial wave pools.

Ocean coastlines are usually the best surfing spots because the swells are the biggest. But surfers don't have to live near the sea to **shred** a wave. Technology makes it possible to create "artificial waves" in pools far away from coastal areas.

Not all surfing takes place in warm waters. In the UK waters are often chilly but some brave surfers even surf during winter! Fortunately, surfers can endure cold water by wearing **wet suits**. Hardcore surfers debate where the best waves can be found – California, Hawaii or Australia.

shred surfing the waves successfully
wet suit close-fitting suit made of material that keeps athletes warm in cold water

Visual glossary

wax
Surfers rub wax onto their boards. The wax helps them grip the board with their feet while they're riding waves.

earplugs
Surfers in cold water use earplugs to prevent Surfer's Ear, a condition that causes bone growth in ears.

sunscreen
Surfers should always apply sunscreen before going outdoors. Sunscreen helps protect the skin from sun damage.

SUN SCREEN SPF 30 SUN PROTECTION CREAM

dry bag
A dry bag is an essential piece of gear for surfers. It's used to store wet towels and suits.

board
The size of a surfboard depends on the individual surfer's height, weight and experience level. In general, a beginner's surfboard should be about 90 centimetres taller than the surfer.

fins
Surf fins attached to the bottom of a surfboard provide stability and improve performance. There are multiple options for fins: single-fin, twin-fin, thruster, quad and five-fin setups.

wet suit
Without the comforts of a wet suit, many surfers simply couldn't stay in the water very long.

leg rope
In case of a fall or accident, a leg rope connected to the surfer's ankle ensures a board doesn't float away from its owner.

13

CHAPTER 3

Wakeboarding

Wakeboarding is a powerful mix between water skiing, surfing and skateboarding. Wakeboarding is most similar to waterskiing. It involves being pulled by a **motorboat** to travel over the water. However, instead of skis, this sport uses one wide board. A wakeboarder holds on to a rope attached to a boat. As the boat moves, the athlete uses its **wake** for extreme boarding.

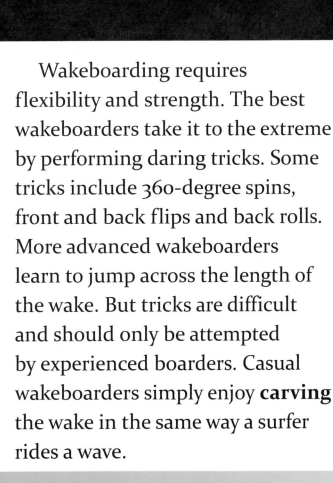

Wakeboarding requires flexibility and strength. The best wakeboarders take it to the extreme by performing daring tricks. Some tricks include 360-degree spins, front and back flips and back rolls. More advanced wakeboarders learn to jump across the length of the wake. But tricks are difficult and should only be attempted by experienced boarders. Casual wakeboarders simply enjoy **carving** the wake in the same way a surfer rides a wave.

Every year more than 4 million people strap on a board, grab a rope and glide across the water on a wakeboard.

motorboat fast, medium-sized boat that is moved by a motor
wake V-shaped trail of waves left behind a moving boat
carve make sharp turns on a wake or wave; can be used to describe surfing or wakeboarding

Wakeboarding began as a combination of surfing and waterskiing. While the board might look a little bit like a surfboard, a wakeboard does not require big waves. It just needs the wake created by the boat.

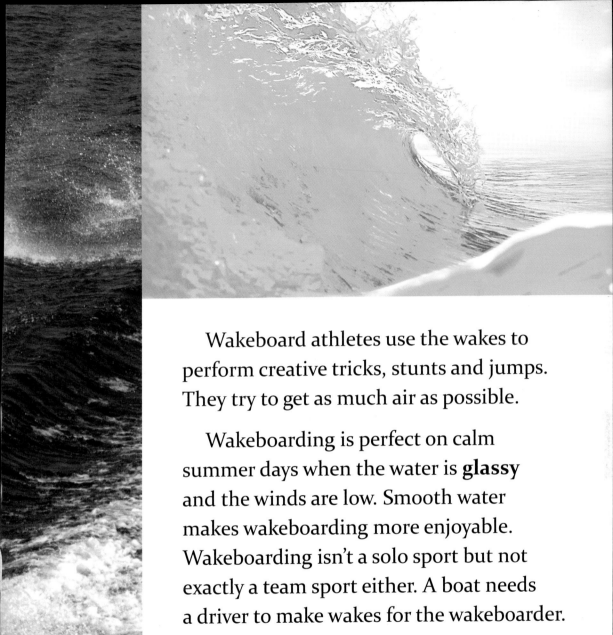

Wakeboard athletes use the wakes to perform creative tricks, stunts and jumps. They try to get as much air as possible.

Wakeboarding is perfect on calm summer days when the water is **glassy** and the winds are low. Smooth water makes wakeboarding more enjoyable. Wakeboarding isn't a solo sport but not exactly a team sport either. A boat needs a driver to make wakes for the wakeboarder.

glassy smooth, calm water; wakeboarders want the water to be as glassy as possible

CHAPTER 4

Windsurfing

In some water sports, like wakeboarding, the wind is no friend to an athlete. Windsurfers have the opposite attitude. Windsurfers rely on steady winds for their natural thrills. The ideal wind speeds for windsurfing range from about 10 knots for beginners up to 20 to 30 knots for advanced windsurfers.

Windsurfing combines parts of surfing and sailing. People first began windsurfing in the late 1950s. By the 1970s, it had become popular in North America and Europe. People wanted to show off their skills and find out who was the best. The first world championships were held in 1973. Today windsurfing is an event in the Olympic Games.

Freestyle sailors try to perform the most daring tricks. They ride huge waves and get big air when they do jumps. Racing sailors use wind power to reach top speeds. **Slalom** windsurfing is similar to racing, but it also involves skilfully moving around **obstacles**.

slalom   move or race in a winding path, avoiding obstacles
obstacle   object or barrier that competitors must avoid during a race

Windsurfing became a popular extreme water sport with numerous categories: slalom, big air, speed sailing, freestyle and more.

Windsurfing attracts water sport athletes, from the casual to fanatical. Water sport athletes of all ages windsurf. Children as young as five years old can start windsurfing by using lightweight **sailboards**. Teenagers have even won world windsurfing championships.

sailboard wind-powered surfboard with a sail mounted on a joint

A breezy day can cause problems for some water sport athletes. For windsurfers, when the winds pick up, it's time to get out on the water.

CHAPTER 5

Cliff diving

Surfing, wakeboarding and windsurfing are popular, but cliff diving is one of the original extreme water sports. Cliff diving began in Hawaii in the 1700s. Hawaiians call cliff diving *lele kawa*, which means "entry with no splash". Cannonballing in cliff diving is a recipe for disaster. The best cliff dives leave hardly any splash. To this day, Native Hawaiians continue honouring their cliff diving history.

A man cliff dives from the Waimea Falls in Oahu, Hawaii.

Cliff diving is the most natural of extreme water sports. A diver launches into the air with a series of twists and turns before entering the water. But cliff diving is also dangerous and intense. Jumping off a steep cliff is a daring act.

Cliffs are near bodies of fresh and salt water. Most divers have experience high diving into pools. The only equipment a cliff diver needs is a bathing suit. Even jumping into the water in a **pencil dive** is risky. That's why most cliff divers never dive alone. They use the **buddy system**. The World High Diving Federation says dives higher than 20 metres should have rescue divers nearby.

pencil dive feet-first dive in which the diver makes the body as straight as a pencil
buddy system pairing up with a partner to ensure each other's safety

A cliff diving athlete jumps from a 21-metre high platform during the Red Bull Cliff Diving World Series in Switzerland in 2018.

The Red Bull Cliff Diving World Series has raised the sport's profile. The diving series includes locations featuring lakes, oceans, quarries, cities and historical landmarks. In 2019, a Cliff Diving World Series event was held in Raouché, Lebanon. Athletes dived off the Pigeon Rocks, which are ancient limestone rocks 27 metres above the sea.

At heights up to 28 metres, World Series divers travel at speeds of roughly 85 kilometers (53 miles) per hour. The divers stay in the air for about three seconds before hitting the water. When landing, a diver's impact with the water's surface resembles a bomb exploding. Divers learn to spread their arms once entering the water. This helps decrease their speed and keeps them from going too deep into the water.

CHAPTER 6

How to make a start

Water sport athletes should be good swimmers. Anyone who wants to become a water sport athlete should master swimming. Young athletes should always have an adult with them when they are near or in water. All athletes, new or experienced, should wear the proper safety equipment.

Water sport athletes constantly risk injury. Bodies of water react to weather in mysterious ways. Lakes and oceans are more dangerous than a pool or playground. Swimmers learn to respect the ocean's power and never let their guard down. Being aware of your surroundings is key to survival.

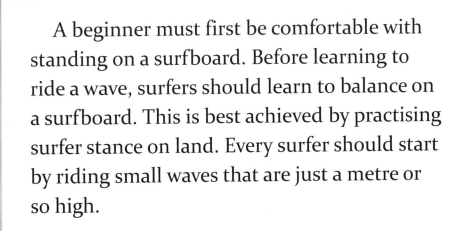

A beginner must first be comfortable with standing on a surfboard. Before learning to ride a wave, surfers should learn to balance on a surfboard. This is best achieved by practising surfer stance on land. Every surfer should start by riding small waves that are just a metre or so high.

Beginner surfers practise a surfing stance on land before getting into the water.

Similar to surfing, windsurfing beginners should focus on learning to balance on a board. Beginners can start with a large board with a small triangular sail. Sailing on lakes with low wind speeds is the best way for beginner windsurfers to learn.

Keep it simple, take it slow and always look out in front of you. Distraction is a recipe for a face-first **wipeout**. But don't be afraid to fall – everyone does!

There is a lot to look at out on the water, but it is important to stay focused.

wipeout fall or crash

GLOSSARY

buddy system pairing up with a partner to ensure each other's safety

carve make sharp turns on a on a wake or wave; can be used to describe surfing or wakeboarding

glassy smooth, calm water; wakeboarders want the water to be as glassy as possible

gnarly large, nasty

motorboat fast, medium-sized boat that is moved by a motor

obstacle object or barrier that competitors must avoid during a race

pencil dive feet-first dive in which the diver makes the body as straight as a pencil

sailboard wind-powered surfboard with a sail mounted on a joint

shred surfing the waves successfully

slalom move or race in a winding path, avoiding obstacles

swell large wave with a long, continuous crest

wake V-shaped trail of waves left behind a moving boat

wet suit close-fitting suit made of material that keeps athletes warm in cold water

wipeout fall or crash

FIND OUT MORE

BOOKS

Extreme Water Sports (Sports to the Extreme),
Erin K. Butler (Raintree, 2017)

*The Science Behind Swimming, Diving and Other Water
Sports* (Science of the Summer Olympics),
Amanda Lanser (Raintree, 2017)

WEBSITE

https://rnli.org/safety/choose-your-activity/surfing
Find out more about how to surf safely and download a guide to
surfsport safety.

INDEX

boards 8, 9, 12, 13, 14, 16, 20, 27, 28

cliff diving 22, 23, 25

competitions 4, 11, 18, 19, 20, 25

equipment 8, 11, 12, 13, 14, 23, 26

Koxa, Rodrigo 4, 5, 6, 7

safety 8, 12, 23, 26, 28

speeds 18, 20, 25, 28

surfing 4, 5, 6, 7, 8, 9, 11, 12, 13, 14, 15, 16, 18, 22, 27, 28

swimming 26

technology 11

tricks 15, 17, 19

wakeboarding 14, 15, 16, 17, 18, 22

waves 4, 5, 6, 8, 9, 11, 12, 14, 15, 16, 17, 19, 27

windsurfing 18, 19, 20, 22, 28

world records 5, 7, 11